Maple

Lori Nichols

Nancy Paulsen Books · An Imprint of Penguin Group (USA)

For Harper, Zoe and Bella

NANCY PAULSEN BOOKS
Published by the Penguin Group
Penguin Group (USA) LLC
375 Hudson Street, New York, NY 10014

USA | Canada | UK | Ireland | Australia
New Zealand | India | South Africa | China
penguin.com
A Penguin Random House Company

Library of Congress Cataloging-in-Publication Data
Nichols, Lori, author, illustrator.
Maple / Lori Nichols.
pages cm
Summary: "A nature-loving little girl's favorite playmate is her maple tree, until the day she's surprised with a baby sister"—Provided by publisher.
[1. Maple—Fiction. 2. Trees—Fiction. 3. Friendship—Fiction. 4. Babies—Fiction. 5. Sisters—Fiction.] I. Title.
PZ7.N5413Map 2014
[E]—dc23
2013013715
Manufactured in China.
ISBN 978-0-399-16085-1
Special Markets ISBN 978-0-399-17667-8
3 5 7 9 10 8 6 4 2

Design by Marikka Tamura.
Text set in LTC Kennerley Pro.
The illustrations for this book were rendered in pencil on Mylar and then digitally colored.

This Imagination Library edition is published by Penguin Young Readers, a division of Penguin Random House, exclusively for Dolly Parton's Imagination Library, a not-for-profit program designed to inspire a love of reading and learning, sponsored in part by The Dollywood Foundation. Penguin's trade editions of this work are available wherever books are sold.

Maple loved her name.

When she was still a whisper,
her parents planted a tiny tree in her honor!

And even though
Flavia,
Millie Jane,
Lena,
Lily,
and Constance
were all good names . . .

Maple was the perfect fit.

And as Maple grew . . .

so did her tree.

Sometimes, when Maple was noisy
(which was a lot),
her parents sent her outside to play.
Her tree didn't mind if she was loud.

Maple would sing to her tree . . .

and sway for her tree . . .

and sometimes even pretend to be a tree!

On some days, when the wind was just right,
Maple would simply lie under her tree,
and its leaves would dance just for her.

Then one day, Maple noticed her tree was bare.
Maple was worried her tree might get cold.

So Maple took off her jacket . . .

and gave it to the tree to stay warm.

Sometimes Maple wished she had someone else to play with.
(The tree wasn't very good at throwing snowballs.)

She wondered if the tree felt the same way.

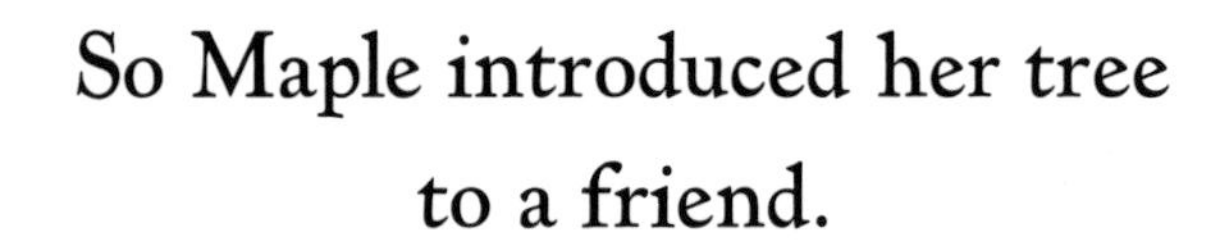

So Maple introduced her tree
to a friend.

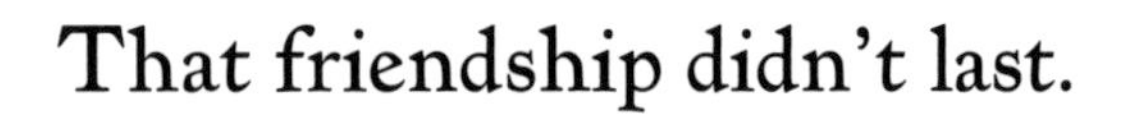

That friendship didn't last.

But Maple and her tree still had each other.

Through winter . . . and spring!

Then one day, something surprising happened.

Then something
really surprising happened.

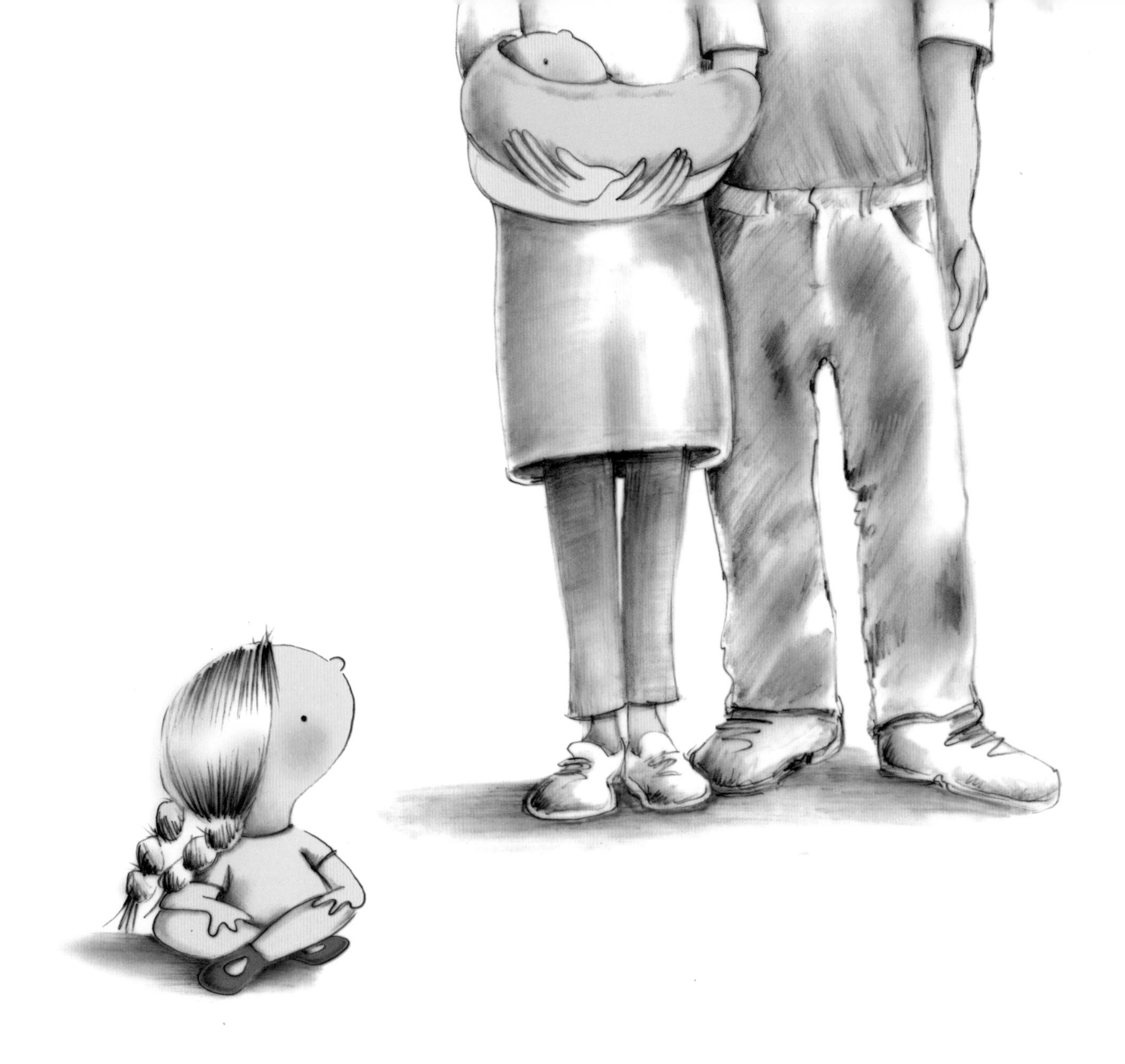

Maple became a big sister.

Maple tried to be a good big sister.

If the baby was cold,
Maple gave the baby her hat and gloves.

If the baby was lonely,
Maple would share her special friends.

But Maple couldn't always
make the baby happy.

And when the baby was noisy
(which was a lot),
Maple would take her outside to play.

And something magical happened.

Maple's tree danced for them both . . .

and there was just enough room under the tree
for Maple and her little sister . . . Willow.